For my dear sister, Lia.

A safe journey, wherever you are.

Leo Timmers
FRANKY

Translated by *Bill Nagelkerke*

GECKO PRESS

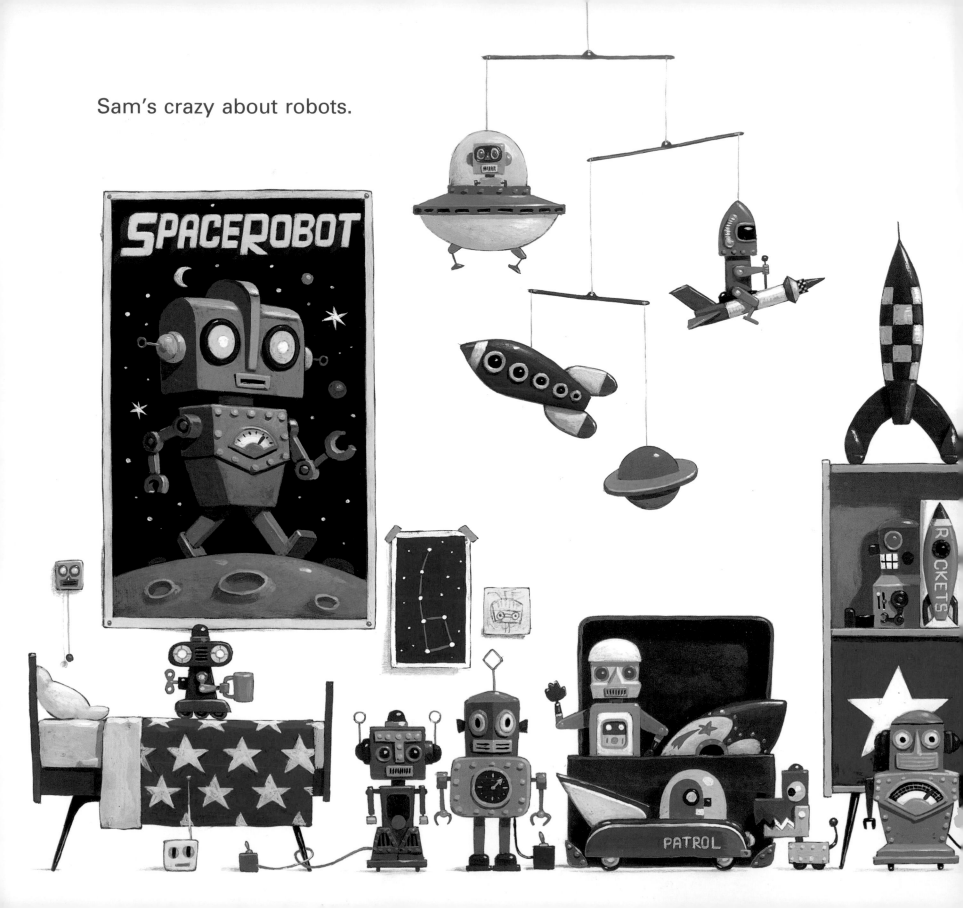

Sam's crazy about robots.

He's sure they live
on a faraway planet.

No one believes him.

One day, Sam had enough.

Franky!

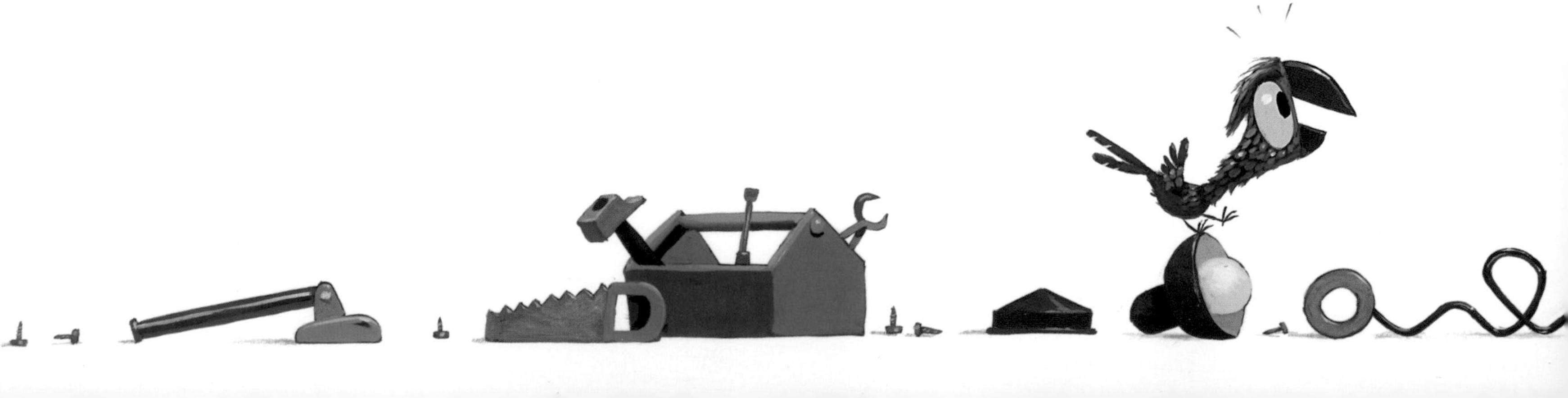

They play robots every day.

Franky is quite sure the robots will visit soon...

...in a big spaceship.

Sam doesn't tell his parents about his new friend.

The weeks fly by.

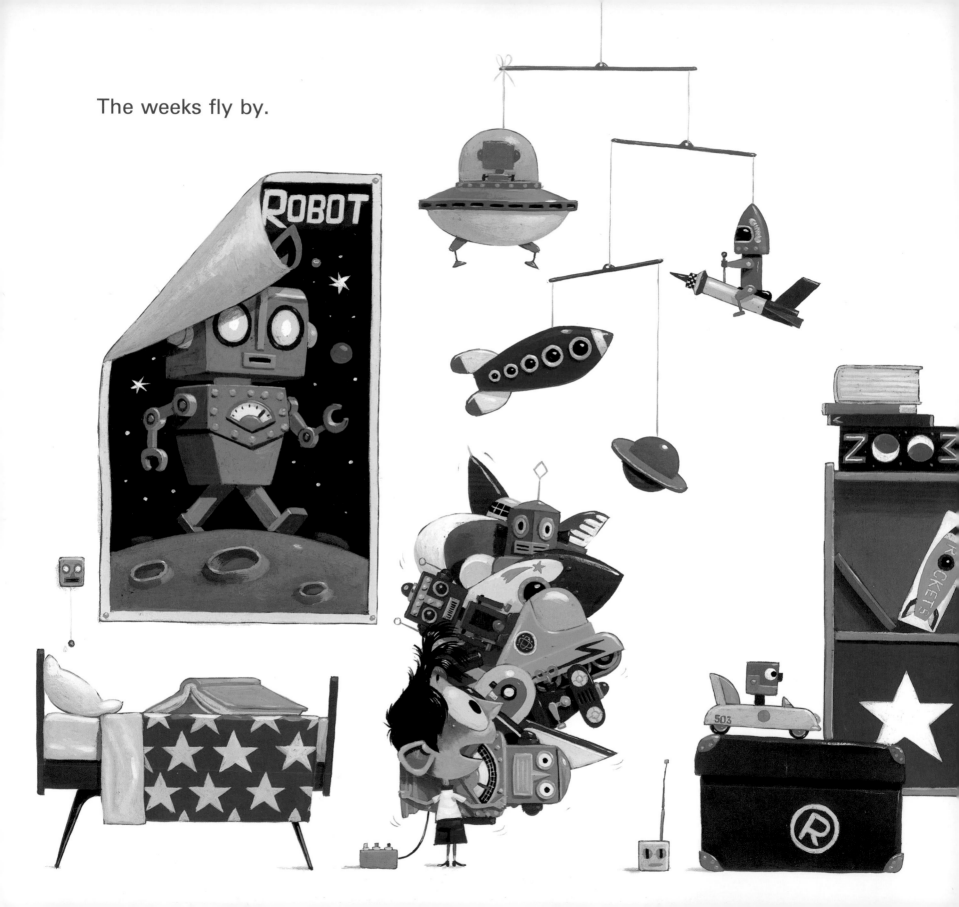

One morning, Franky is quiet.

He doesn't move all day.

Until, in the middle of the night, he wakes Sam.

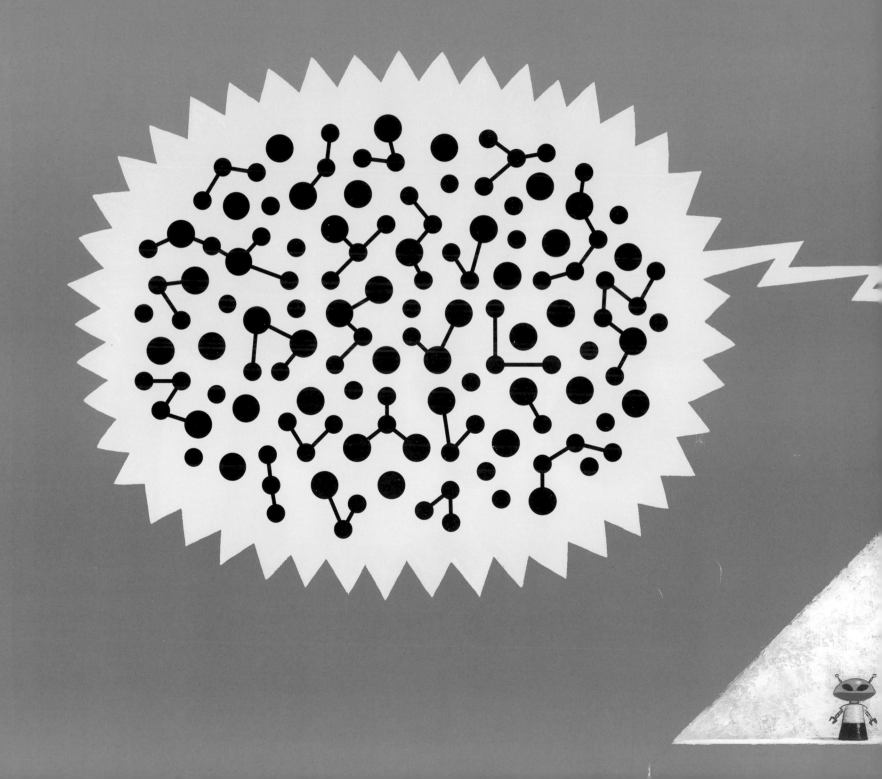

THEY'RE HERE!!

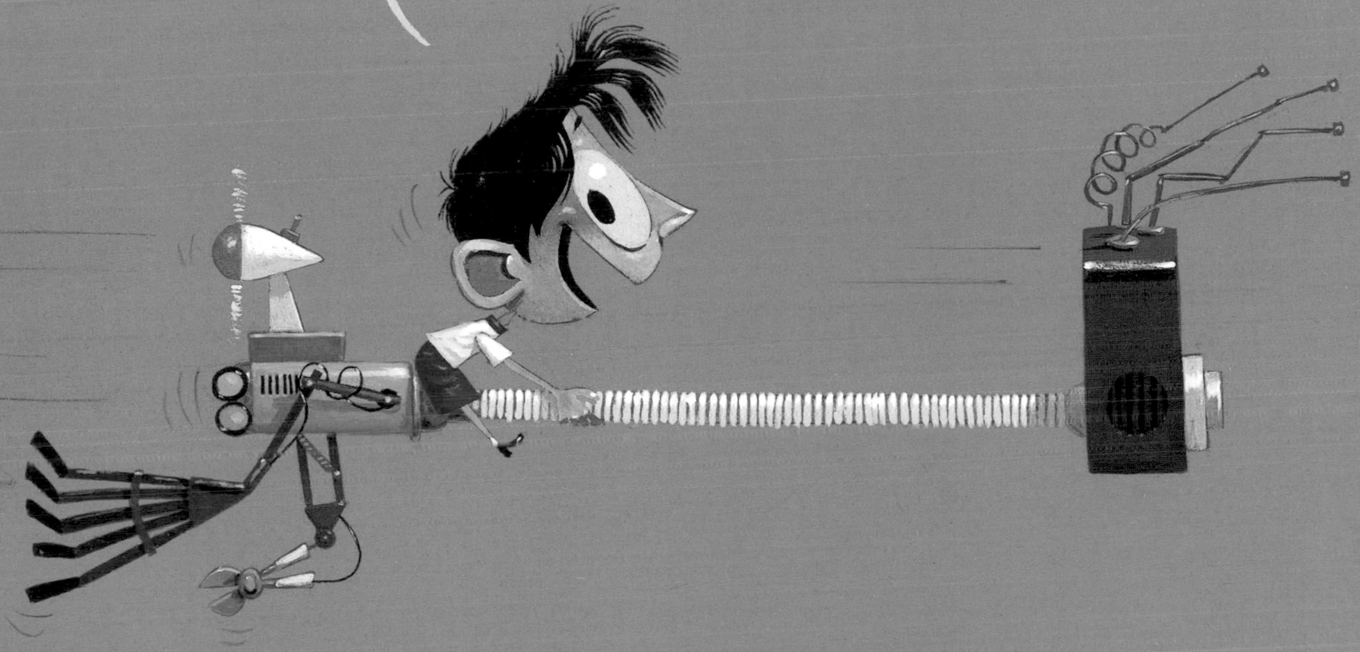

Who?

What?

Sam knows why they've come.

You belong with them.

Take care.

Have fun.

Will you come back?

I'll miss you!

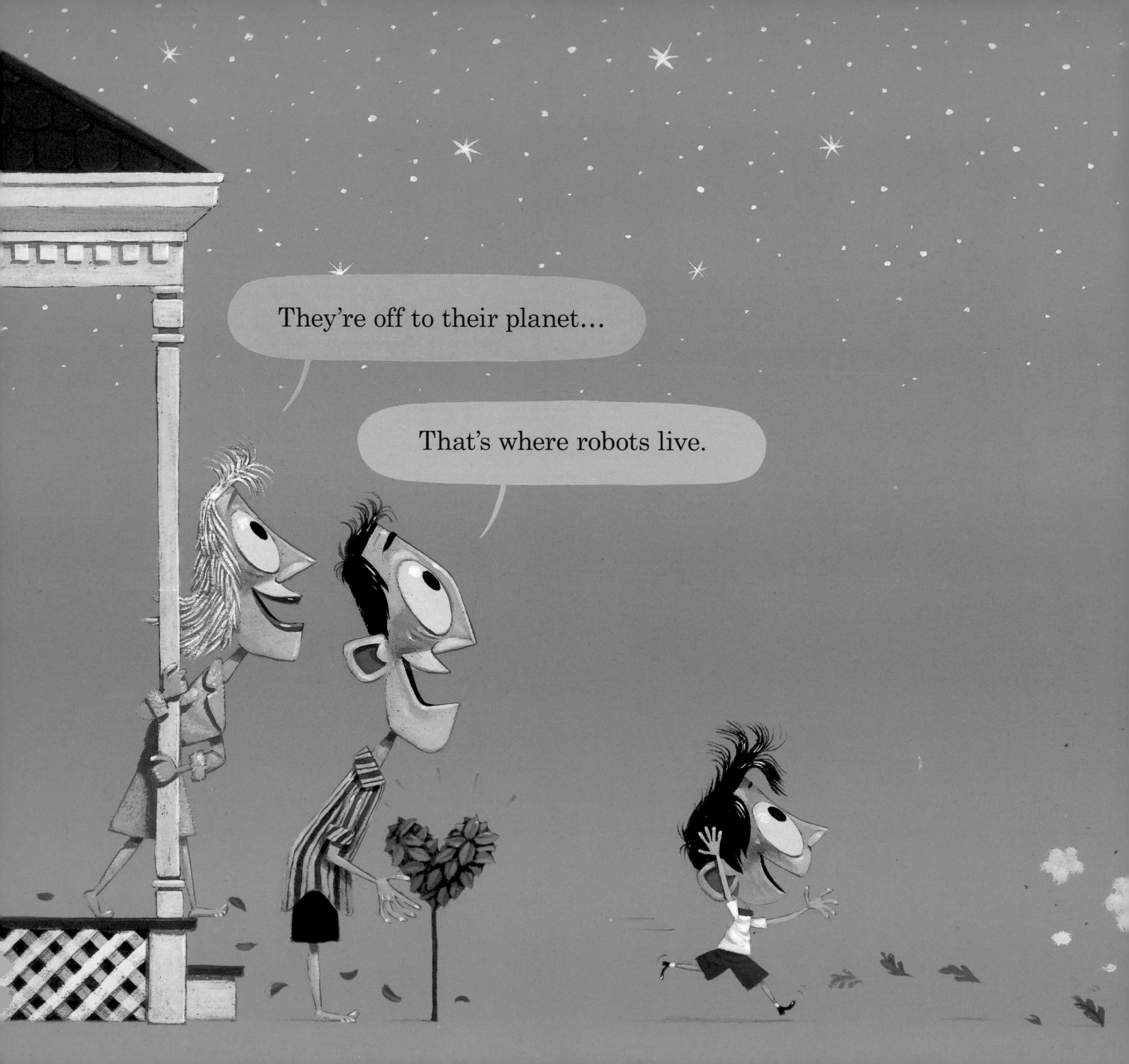
They're off to their planet...
That's where robots live.

Everybody knows that!

This edition first published in 2015 by Gecko Press
PO Box 9335, Marion Square, Wellington 6141, New Zealand
info@geckopress.com

English language edition © Gecko Press Ltd 2015
Copyright text and illustrations © Leo Timmers 2014
Amsterdam, Em. Querido's Uitgeverij B.V

First American edition published in 2016 by Gecko Press USA,
an imprint of Gecko Press Ltd.

A catalog record for this book is available from the US Library of Congress

Distributed in the United States and Canada by Lerner Publishing Group
www.lernerbooks.com

Distributed in the United Kingdom by Bounce Sales and Marketing
www.bouncemarketing.co.uk

Distributed in Australia by Scholastic Australia
www.scholastic.com.au

Distributed in New Zealand by Upstart Distribution
www.upstartpress.co.nz

A catalogue record for this book is available from the
National Library of New Zealand

The translation of this book was funded by the Flemish Literature Fund
www.flemishliterature.be

Translated by Bill Nagelkerke
Typesetting by Vida & Luke Kelly, New Zealand
Printed in China by Everbest Printing Co Ltd,
an accredited ISO 14001 & FSC certified printer

ISBN hardback: 978-1-927271-93-3
ISBN paperback: 978-1-927271-94-0
Ebook available

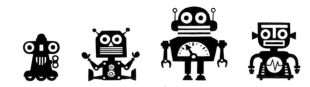

For more curiously good books, visit www.geckopress.com